MONSTER SQUAD
THE BEAST WITH 1000 EYES

BY LAURA DOWER
ILLUSTRATED BY DAVE SCHLAFMAN

GROSSET & DUNLAP
An Imprint of Penguin Group (USA) Inc.

GROSSET & DUNLAP
Published by the Penguin Group
Penguin Group (USA) Inc., 375 Hudson Street, New York, New York 10014, USA
Penguin Group (Canada), 90 Eglinton Avenue East, Suite 700, Toronto, Ontario M4P
2Y3, Canada (a division of Pearson Penguin Canada Inc.)
Penguin Books Ltd., 80 Strand, London WC2R 0RL, England
Penguin Group Ireland, 25 St. Stephen's Green, Dublin 2, Ireland
(a division of Penguin Books Ltd.)
Penguin Group (Australia), 250 Camberwell Road, Camberwell, Victoria 3124,
Australia (a division of Pearson Australia Group Pty. Ltd.)
Penguin Books India Pvt. Ltd., 11 Community Centre,
Panchsheel Park, New Delhi–110 017, India
Penguin Group (NZ), 67 Apollo Drive, Rosedale, North Shore 0632, New Zealand
(a division of Pearson New Zealand Ltd.)
Penguin Books (South Africa) (Pty.) Ltd., 24 Sturdee Avenue,
Rosebank, Johannesburg 2196, South Africa

Penguin Books Ltd., Registered Offices: 80 Strand, London WC2R 0RL, England

Library of Congress Control Number: 2009022925

ISBN 978-0-448-44914-2   10 9 8 7 6 5 4 3 2 1

For Papa.

—Laura Dower

For Steve: My #1 fan, friend,
and twin brother.

—Dave Schlafman

Acknowledgments:
To St. Joseph's fourth-grade class,
who never met a fairy-tale writing
assignment they didn't like: Noël,
Estelle, Alena, Claire, Aidan,
John, & Jack.

TABLE OF CONTENTS

I was in the car on the way to my Tuesday night karate class with Mom and all I could think about was this crazy dream I had the night before.

In the dream, I ran up this mountain that looked a lot like Nerve Mountain here in Riddle. Someone was watching me; I could feel it. I ran faster and faster and faster until—*whammo*!—I tripped and fell into this prickly bush. I picked myself up out of the bush, but just as I was about to make my clean getaway, my left foot got wedged between two rocks! I tried and tried to pull it out, but it wouldn't budge. And then a low, eerie moaning sound filled the air. A giant shadow loomed over me. Quickly, I glanced up and realized (just as quickly) that I was standing eye to eye with . . .

Eeeeeew!

There were at least one thousand oooey, gooey, squishy, squashy, bloodshot eyeballs staring right at me! I jumped up into the air and twisted around— ready to kick. Unfortunately, before I could scissor my legs, my body got heavier and heavier and eventually I couldn't . . .

"HOLY SMOKES! I CAN'T MOOOOOOOVE!"

All at once, I woke up, gasping for air. My bedroom was so dark, but then I saw the shimmery outline of my stuffed snake collection at the foot of my bed.

I was not dreaming anymore. I was home in the middle of Riddle. Everything was back to normal; or at least *normal* for Riddle, which really wasn't saying much.

Riddle is, after all, home to some pretty weird stuff.

There's the three-legged dog at the library that growls at kids who have overdue books. There's the seriously haunted Petroglyph Mall.

And then there's Oswald Leery, B-Monster movie director, who lives way up on Nerve Mountain in his very own fortress. Leery Castle is this creepy-cool place with turrets and hidden passageways and loads of secrets.

Once upon a time, Leery discovered that when someone watched one of his original B-Monster movie reels, a B-Monster would escape from that scary movie world into the real world. Leery and his associate Walter Block tried to capture escaped B-Monsters, but they just didn't have the muscle or instinct to get the job done on their own. They needed help! So Leery got a brilliant idea: Gather up a team of kids to catch the monsters on the loose. He called it the Monster Squad and handpicked four of us to be in the group: me, Lindsey Gomez, Jesse Ranger, and Damon Molloy. We're all in the fifth grade together at Riddle Elementary. When we're not studying, it's our job to blast, stomp, or vaporize escaped B-Monsters into oblivion.

Of course it made perfect sense that Leery wanted me to be in the Monster Squad. After all, I'm smart and most kids at school already call me Ninja. Plus, I have serious, *personal* connections to the B-Monsters. I've seen all of Leery's B-Monster movies at least twice. I have a collection of *B-Monster Galaxy* magazines. I'm even *related* to one of the actresses who appeared in the movies. My Great Aunt San San acted in at least sixty-three of them.

And now I was having dreams about them. The weird thing was, I never even saw a movie with the B-Monster from my dream. I had only seen him once or maybe twice—in photographs from my mom's photo album.

Mom has all these old photos of my Aunt San San, and I think that monster was in a few of them.

Still, it was so random to have dreamed about a monster I'd never even thought about. I couldn't help but wonder if it was a sign.

Mom floored the gas pedal and I jerked forward. She barely made it through a yellow light and we swerved into the parking lot at Dojo Academy with a loud squeal. Through our car window, I saw the other kids in my class head through the glass doors to the karate school.

"See ya, Mom," I said, grabbing my stuff, and hopping out of the car.

As I zipped into the building, the woman behind the big, curved oak desk (I fondly call her Front Desk Lady) shot me a look.

"Karateka!" she barked. "Geiko! Go! GEIKO!"

Geiko means practice and mine was starting right then so there was no time to waste. Quickly, I dumped my grappling bag on the floor and unpacked my ear guards.

Grappling is way more than just karate kicks and chops. It includes some seriously complicated—and dangerous—wrestling moves. That's why we wear all the protective equipment. Sensei, the head teacher at Dojo Academy, is a firm believer in safety.

Since I've been taking karate lessons from the time I was four, I've worked my way up the ranks through blue, green, orange, and red belts. Now I'm *this close* to getting my black belt. Sensei says he thinks I'm almost there, but I have to do well at the Dojo Academy Karate Invitational next week. Here's the rule: At Dojo Academy, no one under age thirteen has ever been permitted to get the black belt. I think I may be the very first eleven-year-old to do it. Fingers crossed.

"Kiiiiiiiiya!"

I bared my teeth and furrowed my eyebrows in the mirror. I had to look as tough as possible to succeed in this class.

"Kiiiiiiiiya!"

"Less wolf, more tiger," Sensei whispered as he passed behind me. "Nice effort."

I nodded and took a deep breath. Then I threw my arms up.

Chut-chut-chut-chut.

My hands chopped at the air like a propeller.

"Hey, Min! Not like that!" shouted an annoying but familiar voice.

"Brick! I didn't see you there."

"Nice helicopter imitation, Min. Can you do seaplanes, too?"

"Sure, laugh at my moves," I grumbled. "At least I'm practicing. Meanwhile, you're just taking up space."

Brick laughed. His real name is Sebastian, but everyone has called him Brick since last year. He is the only sixth-grader I've ever met with genuine biceps. (And I only know this because he flexes them at me all the time.) He got the nickname Brick when he unsuccessfully tried to break a block of wood with his head and had to get twenty-three stitches. Everyone started saying he had bricks for brains and, eventually, they just started calling him Brick. He doesn't care, though. He wears that scar like a badge of honor and he's probably just as proud of his nickname.

Brick is always telling the rest of the karate students what to do; me most of all. It can be annoying—except for the fact that he's usually right on.

"Karateka!"

Sensei clapped and came to the front of the class to get things started.

"Osu," Sensei calmly said after we'd all lined up.

Everyone bowed back. "Osu," we all said, except for Brick.

Brick just thinks *osu* is a joke. He doesn't really have respect for karate as an art form. He just does it because he gets to show off.

"Osu *what*, Stella?" he always jokes. "Oh soooooo . . . glad to meet you?"

I hate that lame joke!

Osu is important. Sensei taught us that. It's the Japanese word for patience, determination, and perseverance. Brick doesn't have any of those.

Sensei clapped again and asked Brick to demonstrate a kick for the rest of us.

He stood very silent for a moment and then, in a burst of energy, kicked so hard, his entire body flew through the air.

Even I was impressed.

"Nice footwork," Sensei said. "Stella, why don't you demonstrate the same kick?"

I stared at Sensei but did not move. I felt my cheeks turn red. Then I remembered my dream. Even in the dream, I was about to thrust a powerful kick into the air—and I couldn't do it.

What did it mean?

Somehow, I knew that mastering that kick was very important. It would get me my black belt, make me a star in Sensei's eyes, and maybe even help me get the B-Monster.

I, Stella Min, also known as the Ninja, needed to figure out how to make it really happen.

B-MONSTER
BET

Wednesday morning, I was heading to the Monster Squad's usual table at the back of the cafeteria when something hit my head.

It was a piece of pepperoni.

A moment later, Damon sped by with his tray. That boy was armed and dangerous on pizza day.

"Hey, Stella," Lindsey said to me when I came to the table. "I can't believe you got the macaroni and cheese. It glows in the dark."

I stared down at my lunch tray and shrugged. "I don't care if it's radioactive yellow, I'm hungry," I said defiantly.

As I slid in beside Jesse, he turned to me. "We were just talking about the B-Monsters," Jesse said. "Which one do you think is next?"

Interesting timing, I thought. *Maybe my dream last night really was a clue.*

"Last night, Dad and I watched *Zattack of the Zombies*, which was awesome as usual, followed by the digital, re-mastered version of *They Came from Planet Q*, including super-scary deleted scenes! I wonder if it's one of them?"

"Those extra scenes aren't scary," Damon

groaned. "They're lame-o. Those robots from Planet Q are for babies!"

"Molloy," Lindsey warned. "Don't be rude."

"I can't help myself," Damon said. He scratched his head. "Now if you want *really* scary B-monsters, how about the Martians from *Martian Mayhem*? Or that mega-beast from *Tuskadon*? And don't forget the alien plant life in *Wait Until the Earth Explodes*. That's classic."

"Classic? You have got to be kidding!" Lindsey blurted. "*Explodes* is the dumbest B ever made."

They were all getting so off topic and I actually had something relevant to add. I leaned in and whispered, "I dreamed about a B-Monster last night."

Everyone stared at me. I took in a big breath because I was afraid that what I was about to tell them would sound really crazy.

"No way!" Lindsey said. "Where was it from? What was its name?"

I shrugged. "I don't know for sure. It had something like one thousand blinking eyeballs," I said. "And it could move surprisingly fast. It made terrible squishing noises when it moved."

"Well," Jesse said thoughtfully, "sounds a little like Señor Cyclops, but that B-Monster only has *one* creepy eyeball, not a thousand. And Señor moved super slow."

"Hold up!" Damon said. He pulled a very crumpled piece of paper out of his pocket. He keeps this running list of B-Monsters in his pocket for exactly this purpose!

He's like the B-Encyclopedia.

Chomp-O the Magnificent
Rodiak
Señor Cyclops
The Weirds
Space Leech
Dr. Doom
Slimo
Tentacular
The Worm-Bots
Robototron
Mega Mantis
50-Foot Ice Beasts
The Zombies
Smog Thing
Beast with 1000 Eyes

"That's it!" I cried when he read the last name on the list. I remembered seeing the name '*Beast with 1000 Eyes*' on the back of one of Mom's photographs of San San.

"Whoa!" Damon said. "The B-monster is from *The Beast with 1000 Eyes*. But that's impossible. The movie was never released."

"And if an original reel was never released, then according to the rules Leery gave us, the monster could not come back to life, right?" Lindsey observed.

"Not necessarily," I said. "An original reel could still be viewed even if it never was shown in a theater."

"So what are you saying, Stella? Do you think *you* can predict the next B-Monster coming to Riddle from some dumb dream?" Damon cracked. "What are you, B-Monster psychic?"

"Damon, stop being so obnoxious!" Lindsey cried.

"I'm not!" Damon went on. "I'm just saying that if we were B-Monster psychics, Leery would have told us that! And he would not make us do research every time there was a new B-Monster in town. We'd just magically 'know' how to eliminate the monsters."

"I don't know if we're all psychics. But I still think dreaming about the B-Monster with the eyeballs means *something*."

"Yeah, it means you have monsters on the brain. That's just a side effect of being in the Monster Squad," Damon said.

"Maybe the dream isn't psychic," Jesse said. "But it could still be a hint. We could investigate this Eyeball Beast and see where it takes us . . ."

"Yeah! I think we *should* look into it," Lindsey added. "Tomorrow after school, let's head up to Leery Castle to see what Walter and Leery know about this monster."

"Fine," Damon groaned. "But I won't believe the B-Monster is here unless we get real proof."

"Proof like what?" Lindsey asked. "Walking, talking eyeballs?"

"Yes!" Damon said. "And lots of them."

CHAPTER 2

CALLING DR. LEERY

After school on Thursday, the four of us met in the school parking lot and headed to the Nerve Mountain bus stop for our trip up to the castle.

As we rode the bus, sunlight dimmed outside and everything was bathed in a funny, yellow light. I could just make out the top of the castle turrets as we rounded a bend in the road.

"Do you think Leery will even be home today?" Jesse asked.

"Doubtful," I said.

We'd already gotten very used to the fact that Oswald Leery was usually out of town. *Way* out of town. He spoke to us via videophone or online news feeds. No one in the Monster Squad had ever met the guy face-to-face.

When we got to our stop, we jumped off the bus

and headed toward the massive gates that circle the castle grounds. We call these gates Crabzilla gates because they have the Crabzilla B-Monster carved into them. We punched in the old password MANTIS from our previous B adventure. It still worked. That meant that Walter and Leery couldn't have seen the new B-Monster yet. The password only changes once the next monster has been identified.

"Stella! Damon! Lindsey! Jesse! Is that *you*?" Walter shouted from the front door. He had seen us coming on his security cameras. "What on Earth are you doing here?"

"We need to ask you about the next B-Monster," I said. Walter looked confused. "Next B-Monster? Already? I'm not sure how much I can tell you, especially with Dr. Leery being in Antarctica right now . . ."

"Antarctica?" I laughed out loud. I never thought of Antarctica as a place people actually went to before.

"Come in! Come in!" Walter said. "Let's talk inside!"

We briskly followed Walter up to the front door and into the castle.

As soon as we got into the castle, Walter passed around an enormous bowl of cheesy-flavored larva crunch. He made the best snacks.

"So what do you want to know?" Walter asked.

"Stella had this dream," Jesse said. "About a B-Monster we've never seen."

"Yeah, and now she thinks she's B-Monster psychic!" Damon cracked.

"Hmmmm." Walter scratched his chin.

"What does it mean?" I asked.

Walter took a deep breath.

"There is something I need to show you, Monster Squad," he said. He pointed down a long corridor behind him. "I've been waiting for the right time to tell you all about a secret area in the castle. It might help you, Stella, to figure out that dream."

I peered down the hall. I knew the vault was back there.

But what else?

"Dr. Leery calls this the belly of the castle," Walter said as we walked toward it.

I wasn't sure I liked the sound of that, though. *Belly* sounded like we were about to be eaten up.

"Are there other rooms?" I asked.

"Oh yes. Dr. Leery's deepest, most well-hidden tricks are here," Walter said. "Are you kids ready to explore?"

Ready? Was he kidding? I was jumping out of my skin.

"Can I take pictures?" Lindsey asked, holding up her camera.

"As long as you don't show them to anyone besides me, Leery, and your fellow Monster Squadders. What I am about to show you is highly confidential."

"What's here? Do these rooms help to identify which B-Monster will arrive next?" Jesse asked.

"Sort of." Walter shook his head. "Inside these rooms are possible clues. But as Dr. Leery says, the only sure proof of a new B-Monster is acute visual contact."

"A cute *what*?" Damon asked.

"Acute visual contact," Walter said. "That means that a B-Monster must make a public appearance. The members of the Monster Squad can only stop a B-Monster once they've seen him."

As we walked along, Walter led us past the familiar door marked VAULT, the place we'd been many times before to find and watch reels. The cold, stone walls seemed to move in on us a little bit and I tried to think of something un-scary, but my brain kept playing tricks on me.

We passed doors with more dangerous-looking signs like KEEP OUT OR ELSE! and DO NOT ENTER WITHOUT MASK.

"Leery Castle is a tricky place," Walter explained. "Down here, we have a complex series of hidden tunnels and pathways to take us to various rooms, laboratories, and storage compartments. There are more than two hundred rooms here."

"Two hundred rooms?" Jesse cried.

"Whoa," Damon said.

"Don't you get lost?" Lindsey asked.

"No, I have an office with television screens showing me key locations throughout the castle," Walter said. "While Dr. Leery is away, I monitor all of them."

"Hold up! You have Leery Castle TV monitors *everywhere*?" Damon gulped. "So last time we were here and I switched around those pictures on the wall . . ."

"Yes, Damon." Walter made a face. "I saw it."

"Or the time when I fed some larva crunch to Poe?"

"Saw it."

I quickly scanned my memory for any weird things I might have done that could be caught on camera. As I suspected, there weren't any—wouldn't be very ninjalike of me, now would it?

"You are about to pass by some of our most top secret labs inside the castle. Watch your head, the ceilings get low in parts," Walter cautioned as we proceeded down the corridor.

I ducked as we weaved our way, stopping to look at different doors along the hallway.

Lindsey stopped in front of a room that looked like an enormous fish tank. The sign out front said NO SWIMMING. Lindsey was excited at the prospect of going face-to-face with Octo-Blob. She loved those underwater B-Monsters.

But we kept moving.

Jesse got us all to stop at a door that felt cold and slimy. It was actually oozing a little bit around the edges. We knew right away what was in there: leeches! In fact, a small sign on the door gave it away: NO SALT AT ANY TIME. Of course, salt was a leech's worst enemy. In the classic *Space Leech*, scientists transport the leeches and abandon them on a planet made entirely of salt crystals.

A few feet away from the leeches, we saw a door that stretched up a full foot higher than Damon. This room was built for a giant! The door sign read BEWARE OF FUR BALLS.

"I bet Rodiak was here," Damon said. "Whoa!" Rodiak was probably the biggest B-Monster ever, like some kind of mutant King Kong, only way furrier and with more teeth.

Walter stepped in and made sure the door to the Rodiak room was dead bolted.

"We don't want to open this one," he warned. "In fact, I wouldn't recommend opening any of the doors without proper supervision. We do experiments in the rooms, but we cannot guarantee the results."

I shuddered a little bit. The whole visit made me jumpy; not that I ever would have admitted my case of nerves to any of the other Monster Squadders.

Slowly, we continued down the hall, until I saw this sign:

I

F Y

O U C

A N R E

D T H I S

T H E N Y O

U A R E O U T

O F   S I G H T

"What's in here?" I asked.

Walter nodded and smiled. "Answers," he said.

He reached into his pocket and produced a ring of at least fifty gold and silver keys. On the ring was a blue and white charm.

It looked exactly like an eyeball!

CHAPTER 3

NINJAS DON'T GET SCARED

"Be very careful!" Walter commanded as he pushed open the door and flicked on the light.

"Aaaaaaaaaaaaaaaaaaaaaaaaaaaaaaaaaaaaaaaaaaaah!"

I screamed so loudly I thought my head might pop off.

Everyone else screamed, too.

Then I took a very big step backward.

The entire room was filled from floor to ceiling with eyeballs in jars.

"Can these eyeballs see me?" I asked Walter nervously.

"No," Walter assured me. "It looks like the eyes can see you, but the eyes are nonfunctioning. They're in formaldehyde. We used them to create our own eyeball monster."

"Talk about surveillance tactics," Lindsey cracked.

Walter had shown us a few jars like this one other time when we battled Mega Mantis. He had some stored in the trunk of the Leery Castle limousine. But that was different. That time, I only saw four or maybe five jars.

There had to be at least four hundred jars in this room—each holding at least one pair of eyes if not more. That made almost one thousand individual eyes swimming around in stinky eye goop!

No matter what Walter said, they were *totally* looking right at me.

Every. Single. One.

"What exactly do you do with all these eyeballs?" Lindsey asked. She peered into one jar. Then Damon grabbed it and shook the jar like a snow globe.

"Don't!" Walter grabbed it back from him. The jar made a *squooshy* noise.

"You know," Lindsey said. "It's like school in here."

"How?" I asked.

"Too many pupils!"

Damon, Jesse, and even Walter cracked up. But I didn't. I was too busy searching for evidence that the Eyeball Beast was on his way.

"For years, we tested the eyeball's ability to blink, and transmit laser beams," Walter explained as he led us around the room. "We tested weapons to destroy the eyeballs, too, but we stopped our research before finishing up *The Beast with 1000 Eyes* because we ran out of money. As far as Oswald Leery was concerned, the Beast with 1000 Eyes would never live to see another day once production was stopped . . .

"So you can imagine my surprise when you came to me with the notion that the Beast with 1000 Eyes is on the loose."

"Where is the reel—the unfinished one?" Jesse asked.

"Oh my goodness," Walter shook his head. "I'm not exactly sure what happened to the reel. That's a good question."

Just then, an alarm sounded from a faraway part of the castle.

Walter flinched. "Oh dear!" he said. "I need to check that alarm. Lately it's been on the fritz. There are so many controls to manage in this castle! I'll be back in a jiffy. Try not to touch anything big, okay, Monster Squad?"

"Yeah, we know," Lindsey joked. "You've got your *eyes* on us. Right?"

Walter sped out and left us in the half-dark eyeball room with the assortment of *squooshing* jars.

"He's probably got security cameras filming us right now," Damon groaned, searching the ceiling.

That place gave me the creeps. I gripped the top

of a chair and repeated a mantra inside my head to keep my cool.

Ninjas don't get scared!

Ninjas don't get scared!

Ninjas don't get scared!

KLUNK!

By mistake, I bonked the chair into a table. A jar rolled onto the floor. Thankfully, it didn't break, but the lid loosened and a little eyeball juice leaked all over the floor.

What a mess!

I grabbed a cloth hanging on the wall and wiped off my hands and the floor.

"Hey, look!" Lindsey cried. By moving the cloth, I'd revealed a poster on the wall. In fact there were posters all over the wall. With all the eyeballs competing for my attention, I'd missed the posters.

Teeny spotlights burned atop the frames. There were classic B posters like Damon's all-time fave, *Martian Mayhem*, and, of course, *Slimo*. There were some other, lesser-known film posters here, too, like *Beneath the Dirt*, a great, early B-Monster Studios movie about killer worms. And then there was a poster for the movie we all wanted to see.

The Beast with 1000 Eyes.

I surveyed the art on the poster. It was the first time I'd really had a good look at the Eyeball Beast. He was nasty. Magenta-pink-skinned and covered (covered!) from head to toe in gross, bulging eyes. He even had eyes on his *heels* . . .

And he was chasing someone—none other than my Great Auntie San San!

CHAPTER 4

AS GROSS
AS IT GETS

"Hey," Lindsey called out. "Why don't we watch the movie? None of us have actually seen it. And I bet we'll learn more if we screen one of the copies. Walter must have a copy in the vault . . ."

"A movie screening is the best kind of research!" Jesse said.

"Okay," I mumbled.

When Walter came back, we followed him toward the vault. He was sure there was a copy of the movie somewhere inside the vault. Of course there were hundreds of reels—mostly copies—scattered around. We scanned shelves for a solid ten minutes before I discovered a stack of movie reels placed on a low shelf. The shelf had not been touched in years; I could tell. It was layered with thick dust and cobwebs. I found reels with peeling labels. Most were marked COPY. Then I found one that was marked THE BEAST WITH 1000 EYES on one sticker with a COPY sticker placed on top.

Jackpot!

I handed the reel to Walter and he popped it directly into the projector. Then he dimmed the screening room lights. The music swelled. The words AN OSWALD LEERY PRODUCTION flashed across the screen.

"This better be good," Damon whined.

The first shot in the film was a close-up of the Eyeball Beast in all of its bloodshot glory, each eyeball shaking and throbbing. I could see spider veins on the whites of all one thousand or more dangling eyeballs. The many eyes were different colors, too: blue, green, hazel, and even pitch-black. The B-Monster had fingertip eyes, too, on its palms; and crazy, blinking fingernails that made noise with each blink.

Sploosh. Sploosh.

There was a lot to be learned by watching this movie. For starters, the Eyeball Beast was not born on some faraway planet or in the middle of a tornado. This B-Monster was made in a laboratory not unlike the labs we had just visited. And when the monster was "born," it was just a lone eyeball that grew and grew and GREW into a cluster of eyeballs—like a seedling grows into a plant.

The Eyeball Beast wasn't a flying bug B-Monster like Mega Mantis or one of those free-roaming B-Monsters, like Slimo. It didn't live in a cave or in the pipes under the sink, either. This B-Monster grew up in the laboratory, where it was poked and prodded by a bunch of kooky scientists looking for answers.

Why did the monster have so many eyes? Was it to see better? Did it have X-ray vision? The scientists poked the beast with needles and paddles and pretty much anything they could get their mitts on but they never were able to find an answer.

And no big surprise, but the beast was very unhappy. One day, it just snapped. All of its googly

eyes opened wide at the same time and it started to blink, and the more it blinked, the more bad things started to happen in Riddle.

The scientists were the beast's first targets. It put them in a coma by blinking at them. Eventually, it busted out of the lab and hit the real world. That was when it saw Iris, my aunt's character, for the first time. The beast chased Iris everywhere, but she never stopped running—not even to catch her breath. This made it mad. It started trashing everything—buildings, roads, machines, and then it did something scarier than anything: It cried. Out of all one thousand eyes.

Next, the beast moved into a movie theater. It seemed to put the moviegoers into a trance just by using its blinking power. The camera panned around the theater. People's eyes glowed, entranced.

And then the beast opened its mouth. I thought for sure it was about to say something. That maybe it would shout, "DIE!" and be super dramatic.

But the monster opened its mouth to speak and instead of words—a giant, bulbous, oozing eye came out of its mouth! It had an eye attached to its tongue!

There are movie monsters who have venomous fangs or sharp, deadly claws. But an eye that pops out of a creature's tongue? That's about as gross as it gets.

All at once, the entire movie theater began to glow, and without warning . . .

Pzzzzzzzffffft.

"Huh?" I cried out in the darkness.

I looked to my left and right. Were the other Monster Squadders still here? What was going on?

Jesse's voice piped up from the dark. "Well, we knew the movie ran out of money . . ."

"Yeah, but we didn't know it would end there! What a scam!" Lindsey said.

My mind raced.

The dream.

The eyeball room.

The tongue. And now . . . Walter swept in and stood up on the little stage. He turned up the lights.

"Look, I don't want to alarm you, kids, but while we were watching the film, I phoned Dr. Leery and told him about your theory. He wants to speak with all of you right away."

LOCKS AND CLOCKS

Walter took us into a small office and asked us to squeeze onto a long sofa. He powered up a large computer and turned up the volume so we could all hear.

"Greetings, Monster Squad," Leery said. "So we meet again."

There was a lot of blustery wind in the background, so we had to lean into the computer in order to see and hear him. "Walter tells me that you believe the Eyeball Beast is the latest monster to hit Riddle. As you now know, this monster starred in a movie that was never shown to the general public. But if you believe that he's rearing his head, and somehow this movie was screened, we have a serious situation."

Up on the videophone, Leery's face was tucked into the hood of a parka, so we could just see his black glasses framed in fur and icicles. In the background were dancing penguins. I think I spotted a polar bear floating on a floe.

"I'll be honest, I have my doubts about the Beast with 1000 Eyes," Leery said, his voice cracking. "But I believe in you, Monster Squad. And if you do end up coming face-to-face with the monster, there are two essential things you must know if you have any chance of beating him."

"First!" Leery said. "The monster is covered with eyeballs—more than a thousand of them. And if he blinks all of his eyeballs at you at the same time, you may be put into a trance or a deep sleep.

"Second! A glance from any or all of these eyeballs could possibly leave a mark on your skin. But fear not! This is only temporary, like an eyeball tattoo. Unless, of course, he glances at you with his primary eye, the one located on his tongue."

I gasped.

"Primary eye?" I cried. "Is that the eye on the tongue from that creepy scene in the movie?"

The image of Leery went to static for a moment and then we watched him push back the hood of his parka and lean closer into the camera again.

"Monster Squad," Leery said, "you have a lot of research to do. Look up eyes and find out how they work. Find out all you can about superstitions related to eyes. There must be answers there! Good luck!"

As soon as Leery signed off, Walter shut down the computer.

"Are you kids clear on what you need to do?" Walter asked.

We all shrugged. Was *anything* ever really clear when it came to Monster Squad?

"So we still haven't even seen the B-Monster up close, right?" Damon said.

"But we're going to assume it's the Eyeball Beast," Jesse said. "We're going to back Stella. We're in this together."

I puffed out my chest a little bit.

"Thanks, Jesse," I finally said, crossing my arms tightly in front of me.

The truth was, there was no harm in investigating now. We could always rule it out later. I was just pleased to *finally* get the support of my fellow Monster Squadders—especially Damon.

After Walter turned off the power in the screening room, he offered to drive us home. It was getting so late! As we rode along, the wheels inside my head started turning, too. I had a genius idea! Walter dropped the others off first. Then he drove to Dojo Academy because I told him I had karate class. I went into the studio like normal, but as soon as I got inside the karate studio locker room, I made a U-turn back to the front desk.

I approached Front Desk Lady.

"May I borrow your Yellow Pages?" I asked.

Front Desk Lady dropped the phone book on the counter with a thud. I flipped through the pages until I got to the letters H, I, J, K, L . . .

Got it!

I had one measly hour before my Mom picked me up—and a ton of work to do. I set my cell phone timer for fifty minutes and hustled outside. There was no time to waste. The air outside was brisk so I walked faster than usual. My destination was 101 Main Street. Within five minutes, I was already staring up at a steel engraved sign: Riddle Towers. What a fancy building! Ornate glass, revolving doors, and a formal-looking doorman standing guard!

I went right up to the guy.

"Is Sandra Lee at home this evening?"

The doorman gave me a bugged-out stare and, for a moment, I worried that I had the wrong address. But then he nodded and reached for the intercom.

"Ms. Lee, you have a visitor . . . *no*, it's not a Grocery Town delivery, it's . . . a young girl."

I fidgeted with the zipper on my jacket. "It's her niece," I said. "Stella Min. Stella *Lee* Min."

I figured our same name might help me get inside. Sure enough, a moment later, a flustered voice came through the speaker.

"Stella?" the voice cracked.

San San! I'd recognize that voice anywhere! It was the voice of a ton of Bs!

I expected the doorman to send me right up to her apartment after that, but then he pulled out this logbook and started asking me all these obscure questions. He called it a "security precaution."

"Are you with anyone?"

"Did you pack your own bags?"

"What is the capital of East Mauritanea?"

For a split second, I felt like I was on *Quizzle*, that game show where you have to answer a series of questions in order to get to the top level and win buckets of cash. Only there was no cash involved here; just an old aunt who wouldn't let me on the elevator. She was more of a hermit than I expected.

The doorman led me to the elevator. "Sorry about the interrogation," he whispered. "She usually doesn't let *anyone* up. She has a lot of locks on her door, too."

"She was a movie star, you know," I said as the elevator door opened.

"You're family, right?"

"Yes," I said, nodding. "How did you know?"

"Are you kidding? You look exactly alike!" the doorman said.

I glanced at my reflection in the mirrored wall near the elevators and smoothed down my hair. She was beautiful, too, of course.

"Thanks for your help," I said as I stepped onto

the elevator. When we got to the penthouse floor, the doors opened onto a wide and empty hall.

"Auntie San San?" I asked, stopping in my tracks. "Hello? Are you here?"

All at once, a flurry of locks twisted and clicked, one after the other. I counted ten in all. Then a door creaked. San San appeared, peering around the side of the door. Her eyes bulged at me.

"Who sent you?" San San called out. She wasn't opening the door any wider to let me inside until I answered.

"No one *sent* me," I said. "I just wanted to see you. I mean, you're my aunt, aren't you?"

"No one comes here unless they want something," San San said before she slammed the door shut again. For a moment, I thought all hope was lost. But then the door reopened—wide.

"I'm sorry," San San said in a hurried voice. "Come in. And hurry."

For a split second, my feet wouldn't move forward. I wasn't nervous because, of course, ninja's don't get nervous. Finally, I was able to go in.

Once inside, I couldn't believe my eyes. It looked a little bit like the rooms in Leery Castle in there, with B-Monster stuff all over the place, crazy rugs all over the floors, and photographs framed on every square inch of wall space.

The objects inside San San's apartment seemed frozen in time. Nothing had been updated since a dozen years ago—or more. The dining room table was covered in dingy, white lace. In the center was a bowl of dusty waxed fruit and a basket of napkins with the initial B. On the wall, I spotted at least a dozen different clocks in the shapes of all the B-Monsters I knew. There was a Crabzilla clock with moving claws that told the time.

It was already twenty after six and class ended at seven. I had to hurry.

"I'm sorry for all this high-end, super spy security," San San said, locking her front door tight—ten times again. "Had to make sure that whoever got off the elevator was the real you. Would you excuse me while I check the doors and windows, too?"

"Why the big lockdown?"

"Just precautions. I need to make sure no one is following me," she answered under her breath.

"Following you?" I asked. "But you haven't gone anywhere in years, right?"

San San sighed. "Oh, I know. But sometimes it feels as if there are eyes out there in the parking lot, in the bushes, looking up at my apartment. I know it's probably just inside my head, but . . ."

"Did you say *eyes*, Auntie San San? Lots and lots of *eyes*?" I asked. "Oh wow. We really need to talk."

CHAPTER 6

LET ME
EXPLAIN . . .

"So why *are* you here, Stella?" San San asked. "I didn't even think you kids knew I existed."

"No, Mom talks about you," I explained. "She told me that she always asked but you never accepted invitations to dinner or holiday celebrations."

"I know. I guess I preferred to be alone all these years. But seeing you now—" she took a deep breath. "This is a nice thing. You remind me of myself when I was your age . . ."

Great Auntie San San had gray hair pulled up in a tight bun, but her face was bright when she spoke.

"Thanks, Auntie San San. You know, I do have an important reason for being here."

San San furrowed her brow. "And what's that?"

"I need to talk to you about Bs."

San San's eyes got wide. "Okay—shoot."

"A few of my classmates and I are B-Monster movie fans," I said, trying not to reveal everything at once. "And we're just . . . well, curious . . . since you were in all the movies. I've seen your name on some posters and in photo albums . . ."

"You want to hear stories about those days in Hollywood?" San San asked as she stood up. "Very well, I can share. Let me show you something."

I settled into my chair. I had a front row seat to the next B, I could feel it in my toes. I was going to get the kind of information I needed to figure out whether the Eyeball Beast was in our midst.

San San came back into the room holding an armful of colored, leather scrapbooks. Each thick volume was bound in leather, bursting with papers and photos. She propped a pile of the scrapbooks in front of me and grinned.

"These are just a few of my life stories," San San said. "From the first Oswald Leery movie to the last. I kept a record of every film."

"Gee," I grinned back. "You know, I've seen all those movies twice and sometimes *three* times," I said.

"Have you?" San San cried. "Well, I'll be a monkey's uncle. You're a real fan!"

I looked down at a red leather scrapbook and cracked it open. The page showed a large photo of San San on a desert island wearing a tribal headdress and strange shoes. The next page showed her, the headdress, and the shoes being devoured by giant scorpions.

I laughed out loud. "*That* must have hurt," I said.

"Not as badly as the time Slimo swallowed me! Heeeee!"

We laughed together. Great Auntie San San's teeth were wide and white enough to be in a toothpaste commercial. I guessed they were probably dentures.

I wanted so much to tell San San that I, too, had been swallowed by Slimo. I was waiting for just the right moment to spill *all* the beans.

"We filmed that island scene on a set, if you can believe it," San San said, showing me some funny photos. "Sometimes I miss the acting days. I miss all the adventure. I've been cooped up here in Riddle Towers for far too long."

San San glanced away, out the window. I glanced at my cell phone timer. Forty minutes left. It was getting late so fast. I could not miss getting back to Dojo Academy in time for my ride with Mom.

"So . . . why did you stop making B-Monster movies?" I asked.

"So many reasons," San San explained.

"Um . . . like what? Did Oswald Leery fire you?" I asked.

"Fire me? Oh noooo!" San San laughed out loud. "Oswald begged me to stay on the films, bless his heart."

"Then why did you stop?" I asked. "You were a superstar!"

"The truth is just too . . ." San San sighed. "Oh, Stella, you wouldn't believe me. Your mother never believed me, either."

"I *will* believe you! I swear!" I exclaimed.

It was time to tell the truth.

"Auntie San San, I've done more than just watch the movies. A few months ago, Oswald Leery came to me and a couple of other kids and asked us to be this group called the Monster Squad. He told us that something weird happened when original B-Monster movies were screened. The monsters started coming to life in Riddle and that B-Monsters are real."

My great aunt's jaw dropped open.

"My cosmic stars, Stella Lee!" she gasped. "How on Earth did you get mixed up in all this?"

"Actually, it was you, Auntie San San," I explained. "Oswald Leery told us that we have this ability to see B-Monsters because someone in our family worked closely with them. For me, it was you. For Jesse, this other kid in the group, it was his grandfather, Max Ranger . . ."

"Max!" San San smiled. "I knew him well!"

All at once, San San's eyes darted around the room. She went pale and looked worried. "What aren't you telling me?" San San asked. "Is there a B-Monster on the loose again? Which one? Is it coming for *me*?"

"Sit down, Auntie San San," I said, trying to calm her down. "Let me explain . . ."

I told San San what we saw inside the castle; and about our fights with Slimo and Mega Mantis. I told her about the other three members of Monster Squad and how annoying Damon usually acted. When I finished telling her all that, I told her about my eyeball monster dream.

She stared, dumbfounded.

"Do you think I'm bananas?" I asked.

San San nodded slowly. "Of course I do, my dear, but aren't we all? I can't believe it has taken us this long to find each other."

She threw her arms out wide and I jumped in for a squeeze. She smelled a little bit like pickles, but I didn't mind. I like pickles.

"Today," I went on, "when I saw the poster for *The Beast with 1000 Eyes* in this secret lab room at the castle, the same monster I saw in my dream,

I got this feeling. I felt like I found the beast—and you—for a reason."

San San reached to the bottom of the scrapbook pile and took out a blue leather album I hadn't seen yet. On the front was a postcard replica of the *The Beast with 1000 Eyes* poster. San San's image was teeny-tiny in the art, but I could still tell it was her.

We flipped through a few of the scrapbook pages together. There were great shots of the monster chasing San San through a swamp, down a dark tunnel, and into a snow-covered valley. "In the movie, the beast fell in love with me and I couldn't shake it," San San explained.

"The Eyeball Beast falling in *love*? Sounds totally gross," I groaned.

"Yes, gross," San San chuckled. "But this was no romance! The beast destroyed everything in its path, put people into trances, and caused floods with its tears, and then—"

Rrrrrrrrring.

San San stopped talking and turned to me with a worried look. "What was that?"

Rrrrrrrrring.

San San scrambled for her door, thinking

someone was outside. I stood up to follow her, because I thought so, too, but then I realized that the ringing was actually coming from my pocket! I pulled out my cell phone.

"Auntie San San! It's just my phone."

The cell phone timer was up.

My time with San San was up.

The last thing I wanted to do was leave, but now I had to race to Dojo Academy before Mom got there first.

CHAPTER 7

YO, WHAT'S WITH THE EYEBALL NECKLACE?

Mom would be picking me up after class—in about ten minutes. There was no time to spare. San San opened the ten locks for me.

"Thank you so much," I gushed on the way out.

"Wait!" San San called out. She ran into the other room. I could hear her throwing open doors and drawers. She came back a moment later and handed me a small, gold box. "I want you to have this, Stella Lee."

I lifted the lid off the box and unwrapped the gold tissue paper inside. There was a necklace.

"It's called an amulet," San San said. "I had it made as a souvenir from *The Beast with 1000 Eyes*. The stone was just one of the beast's prop eyes, but I liked the way it looked. And now I believe the amulet has kept me safe all these years. It's

65

my good luck charm. And now I want to share it with you."

The amulet looked so real, it creeped me out a little. It looked as if it was staring at me, just like the jars of eyeballs in the lab. But it was also beautiful, like a jewel. I could understand why San San kept it all this time—and why she believed in its powers.

We headed out into the hall. San San took me by the shoulders and looked deep into my eyes.

"Stella," San San said in a low voice, "Oswald Leery knew there was a risk when he created the Eyeball Beast. If it ever came to life, it would be very dangerous. Please be extra careful . . ."

I gulped, confused. "Are you saying I shouldn't fight it?"

"No! Fight it! But stay tough! Don't be scared of anything. I may have looked brave up there in the movies, but I was only acting," San San confessed. "Not like you. I can tell, you're the real thing. You have . . . what does Sensei call it?"

"Osu?"

"Yes! Lots of osu!"

The second alert on my cell phone alarm went off.

"Oh! I have to go!" I said.

I pulled the amulet necklace over my head and pressed the elevator button.

"Keep the amulet close to you at all times," San San said. "It will protect you."

Just then the elevator doors opened. I hustled in.

"Kiiiya, Ninja!" San San called to me before the doors closed.

"Kiiiya!" I called back.

When I got back down to the lobby, I raced outside and headed for the karate studio. I felt badly that I'd missed a proper practice. After all, getting the black belt was supposed to be at the top of my "to do" list. But my time with San San was more important right now.

Walking along, I imagined the Eyeball Beast that I'd seen in the movie. My stomach flip-flopped at the thought of all those eyeballs. I kept my head down and my feet in fast forward all the way to Dojo.

Whoooooooooooooo. Was that the wind?

I stopped. "Hello?" I asked the night air.

Whoooooooooooooo. It was the wind.

"Hello?"

My nerves were tingling.

"Hello?" I called out a third time. "Is someone there? I mean it, if you're there please come out right away."

Squooshy. Squooshy. Squooshy.

I looked to the left. I looked to the right. Hold on! The bushes were rustling! There was something here . . . something in the darkness . . .

Then I noticed a faint glow.

The amulet was warm. It was yellow.

Squoooooooooooosh.

Carefully, I leaned closer to the cluster of bushes near the sidewalk where I stood, and then I saw something incredible. There were little white dots of light inside that bush, peering back out at me like . . . eyeballs?

There was no time to think. I had to run, down the block, way past the bushes, all the way to Dojo Academy. It was the Eyeball Beast! For real!

When I flew into the karate studio, I thought I needed to explain what had happened and why I missed class. But Front Desk Lady was busy helping another family. So was Sensei. When Mom honked from outside, I simply flew back out the door.

All the way home, I looked for more eyeballs

staring at me from between branches and bushes along the road, but I didn't see anything again.

I fingered the amulet for luck and kept it on as I slept. The way I figured it, San San's charm would protect me just in case that thing from the bushes showed up in my bedroom in the middle of the night.

The next day, when I dressed for school I kept the amulet on under my shirt. Maybe it would even bring me luck on my science quiz?

I couldn't wait for lunch period. I had soooo much to tell the squad.

Before I could say a word to the squad, however, Damon said, "Yo, what's with the eyeball necklace?"

The amulet was poking out from under my shirt. Lindsey saw it, too.

"Where'd you get *that*?" she asked.

I told the squad about my visit with San San and the amulet.

Then I told them about what I saw in the bushes.

"You saw the B-Monster? For real?" Damon squealed. "It could have been a cat."

"Or fireflies," said Jesse.

"Fireflies and cats don't go 'squooshy, squooshy,'" I said.

"If you end up being right and the new B-Monster does turn out to be the Eyeball Beast, it'll be pretty impressive," Damon said as he raised his palm for a high five. When I went to slap it, he pulled it away at the last second. "*If*," he said.

I'd show him . . .

CHAPTER 8

GLOW AWAY!

I couldn't stop thinking about the Eyeball Beast. Would he show up at school? Would he put the student body into a trance?

During math, I got my answer.

My neck started feeling superhot.

My amulet started to glow again.

What was going on?

As soon as the bell rang, I leaped out of my chair. With one hand, I grabbed the back of Lindsey's sweater on the way out of the classroom. With the other hand, I shoved the necklace under my shirt.

"Meet me in the stairwell. Five minutes. Tell the others," I said. I had to run out of there quickly before someone saw my neck light up like a Christmas tree. But by the time I got to the stairwell, the amulet was back to its dull state. No glow.

"Stella!" Lindsey came busting through the stairwell's steel doors. "What's so urgent?"

Damon and Jesse raced through the doors a moment after that.

I tried to act cool, like I knew *exactly* what was going on, even though I didn't have a clue.

Everyone examined the amulet for me. We passed it around. We all tried it on. It didn't change one bit.

"Why would the amulet start to glow?" Jesse asked aloud.

I thought about the movie and all the things we'd seen so far.

"Maybe it's trying to tell us something," I suggested.

"That's it!" Jesse said. "The glow is a signal. Remember when we fought against Mega Mantis? All those little swarms of bugs would appear before the B-Monster came on the scene?"

We all nodded.

"B-Force!" Lindsey cried. "Of course! Sometimes there is a powerful energy before the

B-Monster shows up. It shows itself in different ways. It could be lots of flying insects . . ."

"Or a glowing amulet!" I cried. The more I thought about it, the more it made sense.

"Wow," I said. "San San told me that she got the eyeball amulet when she was making *The Beast with 1000 Eyes*. It was just a prop she took from the set. After that, it became her lucky charm. But I don't think she knew that it had the power to glow."

The school bell rang loudly. A crew of kids pushed and shoved their way into the stairwell, jostling us as they traveled from their last class. School was over.

"Let's meet in front after school and figure this out," I suggested. "We can stop over at Auntie San San's. Maybe she can help us figure out what makes the amulet glow."

After school, we walked toward Riddle Towers. Lindsey noticed that the amulet's light kept getting brighter and brighter. That wasn't the only change.

"H-O-T!" I cried.

"What's the problem?" Jesse asked.

"How hot can it be?" Damon snapped.

I handed it to Damon but he could hardly handle it, either. It was like we were playing a game of hot potato.

"You hold it!"

"No, you hold it!"

Lindsey finally grabbed the amulet and shoved it inside her camera case.

"I'll hold it," she declared. "Until we get to San San's."

The Monster Squad turned off the main road and headed for a shortcut to the Riddle Towers parking lot. We passed by a fountain and a public garden and then the carousel in the park and we were about to cross over a little stream when Lindsey grabbed my shoulder.

"Stella! Did you see that?" she whispered.

I looked around. "See what?"

"Something in the bushes," she said. "Do you think . . ."

I looked over at a blooming bush. It shook a little bit. *Were* we being followed? The shaking bush started to shake a little bit more and more and then—

"RIT RACK!" something growled at us.

Lindsey and I froze in our tracks.

"Did you hear that?" I asked, but she couldn't say a word. Up ahead, the boys whirled around, too.

"RIVE RIT RACK!" the thing cried out again.

"What *is* that?" Jesse yelled.

"What is it saying?" Lindsey asked. She grabbed for her camera again, but when she unzipped the case, it flew open and the amulet landed on the sidewalk.

Now it was glowing so brightly, it looked like it had batteries inside.

"RIVE RIT RACK!" The noise came again.

The boys rushed back to us. "Let's go!" Jesse shrieked. "Fast!"

"RIVE RIT RACK!"

"What does it mean? What is it saying?" asked Lindsey.

"I don't know—but it's got to be the B-Force again!" I called out as I ran. "It's got to be the Eyeball Beast. He must be right here! The amulet glows brighter as it gets closer to us!"

The squad might not have been convinced yet that it was the Eyeball Beast following us. But I was. It had to be. Between the glowing amulet and my dream, it just fit together.

"What are we supposed to do now?" Damon asked.

"Move it!" I shouted. "Riddle Towers is right over there!"

CHAPTER 9

"RIVE RIT RACK!"

San San's apartment building lobby was empty when we ran inside.

The doorman was not at his post.

I pressed the UP button and waited nervously. I figured that, at any moment, the Eyeball Beast would come bursting through those beautiful glass doors! I sent San San a text message: We're on our way up. Open the door!

When the elevator opened on the penthouse floor, San San was waiting. "Quick! Inside! All of you!" She led us inside and triple-quadruple-locked the door behind her.

"Whoa! Look at this place!" Lindsey cried when she saw all the art on the walls and photographs on the tables. Lindsey snapped off the lens cap on her camera and took a few photos. Even in the midst of a B-Monster crisis, that girl had her camera ready.

"What's going on?" San San asked.

"It's amazing. You guys really do look exactly alike," Lindsey said as she snapped a photo of San San and me.

I guess movie star looks just run in my family.

"Why are you all out of breath?" San San asked.

"Something large and scary sounding was chasing us down Main Street," Damon said.

"What?! What did it look like?" she asked.

"We never got to see it," Lindsey answered.

I pulled the amulet out of my jeans pocket. It wasn't glowing anymore.

I held it up and asked my aunt, "Where did you get this . . . *exactly*?"

"I told you. It was a prop in the movie," she explained. "I used it for a good luck charm."

"How come you never told me that it glowed?" I asked.

"I never knew! It glows?" she asked.

"The amulet glows at certain times," Jesse said. "And its temperature rises, too."

"It gets hot? I've had that for years," San San

79

explained. "It never glowed or got hot for me . . ."

"Never?" I asked. "Ever?"

"Oh dear! I never should have taken it! Give it back to me now and I'll make sure that it gets thrown away—"

"No," I said, holding up the amulet. "We need this charm more now than ever! I think this amulet may be a way to help lead us directly to the Eyeball Beast!"

Jesse explained calmly. "On the way over here, we heard these crazy sounds coming out of a row of bushes," he said. "At the same time, the amulet started to glow like crazy. It was as if the glowing stone and the sound from the bushes were connected."

"Then the beast started to scream at us," Damon said.

San San looked confused. "You *heard* the beast speak?"

She grabbed the scrapbook from *The Beast with 1000 Eyes* and flipped through the pages as if she were looking for clues.

"Oswald Leery never finished the film," San San explained. "But there was a full script. I have it right here."

She fingered through the script.

"Aha!" San San cried.

She read from a scene that had never been filmed. In the director's notes, there was a line: As the monster runs through the streets, the loose eyeball should glow.

"So it *was* B-Force!" Jesse cried.

"Hey, I'd want my eyeball back, too, if it fell out," Lindsey said.

Great Auntie San San sat on one of her sofas and placed her face into her hands. "I'm so sorry, kids. Did all this start when I gave you the amulet, Stella?"

I shook my head. "No. Someone must have screened the original reel of *The Beast with 1000 Eyes*," I explained. "Was it *you*, Auntie San San?"

San San shook her head. "No, no, it wasn't me Stella. I never had a copy of that movie."

All of a sudden, my jeans pocket felt warm. The amulet inside began to burn hotter and hotter. I yanked it out. It was glowing even more brightly than before.

"Egads!" Great Auntie San San said. "It really is alive!"

"The monster must be close," Jesse said.

San San grabbed her chest and began to gasp for air. "It's coming for me!" she said.

"Wait a minute!" Lindsey held up one of the silver-framed antique photos from the dining room shelf. It was a black-and-white picture of San San on the set of *Rodiak*. "Maybe it's coming for you—*and* Stella. You look exactly alike."

San San and I gave each other a quick once-over as if to make sure, one last time, that we looked alike. There was no debate. San San wrapped her arm around my shoulders. "I'm so sorry you had to get involved in all of this!"

"Don't apologize, San San. It's not your fault that the monster thinks I'm you."

"So what now?" San San said. "You need some real help to fight this beast."

"Wait. You can help," Jesse said. "We still have to research ways to destroy the beast, right? Leery always tells us that the more we learn about a monster—"

"The more ways we can figure out how to destroy him," I finished.

"How can I help you?" San San said. Her voice was shaking.

"The script! How was Leery planning to kill the beast before he stopped production on the movie?"

San San flipped back through the script. But the last pages were missing.

San San, her eyebrows knit, was very quiet for a moment. "Wait! I know what to do!" she cried. A thin grin crossed her face. "Leery was very superstitious and often spoke about tempting the evil eye. I bet he built the monster so that it could be vanquished in the same way as the evil eye."

"Yes!" I said. "That's a great lead. We should try and find out everything we know about the evil eye." I raised my arms up with the battle cry, "To the library!"

"No!" San San cried. "We can't go."

"But San San, we *have* to finish this," I said.

"We can't go," San San explained, "because it's too late. The library is closed right now! But it opens up first thing in the morning."

"Tomorrow is Saturday. We can meet there when it opens."

Damon made a face. "Yo, I like to sleep in on the weekend."

"Look, Damon! I've got the biggest karate meet

of my life tomorrow, but I'm still going to help Monster Squad!"

"Aye, eye!" Lindsey quipped. She and her bad puns.

"Meet me at nine o'clock in front of the library," San San said as we headed out to the elevator.

"Double ninja power!" I shouted, just as the doors shut.

BREATHLESS

By 9:06 AM on Saturday morning, the Monster Squad was on the clock. Even Damon "I-Don't-Wake-Up-Until-Noon" Molloy arrived on time.

We had to sort out all the Eyeball Beast mess smartly and quickly. How hard would it be to squash a thousand or so eyeballs?

We swept past Tricks, the three-legged dog, on the library lawn and hustled up the wide, stone steps to the library entrance. San San was there already, huffing and puffing from the climb. It had been a long time since she left her apartment, let alone had to climb a flight of stairs.

"I forgot how beautiful this library is," San San said wistfully as we pushed through the enormous library doors. "And high up! Whew! What a workout!"

San San pointed to the stone surrounding the door. There were gargoyles and some symbols cut into the stone as well as some faces.

"Look there!" San San said.

We all looked up and spied a row of eyes over the door.

"Remember that, wherever you go, someone is always watching you," San San reminded us.

I dreaded the thought of what could have been watching us at that moment.

Inside, the library was dead quiet. The floors were marble and stone, so every footfall, every breath, every single word we spoke amplified like a loudspeaker. Sound bounced around in the entryway like a wonder ball.

Ms. Shenanigans appeared from a side door. She looked surprised.

"My stars! You kids must have gotten up with the roosters! What have I done to deserve a library visit this fine morning?"

Damon cleared his throat. "We need to do a little . . . um, research," he said.

"Research?" Ms. Shenanigans crossed her arms. "What *kind* of research?"

"We need to learn stuff about . . . well . . ." Lindsey stammered.

San San stepped up to Ms. Shenanigans and placed her hand on the librarian's arm. "My dear, we have a situation. We could use the help of an expert . . . and you were the first person we thought to ask."

Ms. Shenanigans smiled. "Oh, well, if you put it that way . . . Where do you need to do the research? The periodicals room? The rare bookstall? How about the—"

"Stacks!" I blurted. I was eager to get going, we were racing against the clock.

"What's your topic?" Ms. Shenanigans asked.

"Superstitions," I said, as if it were the most normal thing of all.

"Hmmm," Ms. Shenanigans scrunched up her nose. "We've got loads of material!"

San San spoke up. "Eyeball superstitions in particular. You know, evil eyes, that sort of thing . . ."

"Well, that's a tall order," Ms. Shenanigans said. "But I love a challenge!"

Ms. Shenanigans led us to a cold staircase that went down to the lower level of the library.

We followed nervously behind in the dark. Then she clicked switches on the wall and the darkness evaporated. Fluorescent light tubes over our heads began to hum. The light burned gray-white. We stepped into a wide, open space packed with books. All those old books smelled musty, like no fresh air had gotten in here for years.

"This place is like a museum!" Jesse said.

I headed for the computers and punched in the words *eye, sight,* and *symbol.* A large book cover image popped up on-screen. It looked like hieroglyphics. There was a picture of an Egyptian holding a scepter. I think he was a pharaoh. In the center of his head was an eye. The title of the book was *Horus, Horses, and Hijinx: Ancient Symbols, Ancient Curses.* It said there was one copy in the Riddle Library stacks.

I called out to Lindsey who ran over to see the book with me.

"Ooooooh! Cool!" Lindsey said. "I know Horus. He is a cool dude with a giant eye on his hand. That book should be in the nonfiction section."

I clicked on the cover again to locate the book's call number. Then Lindsey raced off in search of it.

I glanced at the digital clock on the computer screen: 10:13 AM.

Time was really flying by. I wondered when Ms. Shenanigans would come back.

Kkkkkkkkkkrack.

I shot a look at the stairs. "Hello?" I cried. "Ms. Shenanigans?"

No one responded. I turned back to the books.

Damon ran over with another book covered in green leather. It was coated in a fine layer of dust. He blew some off and cracked the book open. Lindsey and Jesse looked over our shoulders.

Ancient Greeks were very superstitious. They believed a person could cause harm to another person simply by looking at them.

"Great," Jesse said. "So if a stare from a regular person with *two* eyes can cause harm . . . what about *one thousand* eyes?"

"Keep reading, Stella," Damon said. "What else does it say?"

Ancient cultures believed something as simple as a glance from an eye could set a curse on people. And once cursed by an eye or eyes, a person can only break such a spell by doing a few things.

Throw dirty water at the person who has been cursed.

Lick the eyes of the child or adult who has been cursed.

"Aw, those are just gross," Damon mumbled. "Dirty water? Gack! And I'm not licking one thousand eyeballs! Ptttuey!"

"Keep reading!" I said, pointing to another passage, "It says here you can crack a whole egg on a person's head if you want to take away the curse of the evil eye—"

"Okay, so that means we need to come up with a thousand eggs, right?" Lindsey said. "Every one of the curses needs to be multiplied by a thousand in order to work."

All at once, San San appeared from behind one of the stacks, holding up an entirely different book. This one was oversized with a picture of Horus on the front.

"Kids, it says in *this* book," San San continued, "that a person can defeat the power of an evil eye by collecting spit. That spit can then be thrown down onto a cursed person . . ."

"What? Like a SPIT SHOWER?" Damon cried. "Now that's something I can really get into!"

"No wonder Leery couldn't figure out how to

end the movie," Jesse said. "There are too many different ways to fight the evil eye!"

"Why isn't Ms. Shenanigans back yet?" Lindsey wondered aloud. "She said she'd return in a few minutes. It's been more like a half hour."

I glanced up at an old wall clock: 11:10.

"Actually, it's been an hour," I said.

San San opened a thick encyclopedia of myths and read part of a Greek myth aloud to us.

The story was about a cool creature called Argus. Argus was a watchful giant with one hundred eyes; not unlike the Eyeball Beast that was coming after me and Great Auntie San San. Unfortunately, Argus wasn't very lucky. A clever guy named Hermes killed him with a magic wand. The wand sealed off all of Argus's eyes and cut off his head.

"Wow!" I cried. "So what we need is a magic wand like Hermes!"

I reached for the amulet in my pocket. It was warming up.

"Hey, Monster Squad," I started to say.

Out of nowhere, the florescent lights that Ms. Shenanigans had turned on in the stacks all went off at the exact same time.

But there was still light to help us see down there.

The amulet was burning brightly.

"Damon? Stella? Lindsey? Jesse?" Great Auntie San San's voice sounded panicked. "Where are you?"

Squooshy . . . squooshy . . . squissssssssh . . .

"OH NO!" I yelled. "Did you guys hear that? The beast is here!"

Squooshy . . . squooshy . . . squissssssssh . . .

I could barely see my hand in front of my face, let alone another person in the stacks. But I could hear clearly. The sound was way too familiar.

"RIVE RIT RACK!"

"Nooooo! It's here!" I cried. Then I whipped around in a karate pose. "The Eyeball Beast must be in the stacks!"

I heard something move nearby, dodging around the shelves of books. "Monster Squad, where are you?" I yelled out. "Is anyone there?"

"Yes! We're here!" Jesse cried.

Flash! Flash!

Lindsey clicked her camera. The flashes helped us to see better, even for just a little bit.

Flash! Flash!

"Lindsey? Where's the stairwell?"

I spotted an orange EXIT sign at the side of the room. At last we found a way out! Slowly, I moved along a row of bookshelves. I heard something weird way back in the stacks. My eyes had adjusted to the darkness, so I was able to make out a silhouette.

"Run!" I yelled, and pushed the others in front of me. "Move it now before the beast turns us into statues!"

RIVER
OF TEARS

We ran, but the beast caught up.

I nearly fainted when I saw that B-Monster in the icky, oozy flesh.

For starters, it was way more massive than I expected. It was at least eight feet tall! The thousand eyes were incredible! They spun around in different directions like they had minds of their own, blinking out of synch, like stoplights. It made the worst noises ever. What *was* that? And then, as we stood there, stunned by the beast's very presence, it began to blink faster and faster and faster.

"Aaaaaaaaaaaaaaaaaaaaaaaaaaaaaah!"

I threw my arms up and dashed quickly around the monster. The others followed me, screaming. We burst through the door at the top of the library stairs.

"Don't stop! You can't let it blink at you!" I yelled.

"Stella, where are we going?" Jesse asked.

All at once, I heard a *ffffffffffffffft* noise behind us. Of course I thought it was the Eyeball Beast again—hissing now and ready to eat us. But then I realized it was coming from San San. Or at least a can in San San's hand. She sprayed something into the monster's eyes!

"GOTCHA, YA UGLY EYEBALL BEAST!" San San cried.

"RY RANT RY RYEBALL RACK," said the beast.

"What's he saying?" asked San San. "I don't understand!"

Whatever she sprayed slowed down the monster— but only for a moment. It gave us enough time to run through a set of doors onto the library's main floor. The moment we got up there, we noticed something strange.

People in the library were not moving. Not an inch. Everyone was under some spell.

Even Ms. Shenanigans.

She stood by an upstairs display case. She had her hand on another book that I guessed she picked up for us.

I tried to pry the book from her fingers. But she was like stone, trapped in some powerful trance. Somehow I got the book away from her and shoved it inside my bag.

Then I noticed something else.

I had weird black marks on my skin. We all did! The marks looked like eyeballs! Like tattoos of Horus's symbol. During the chase, the Eyeball Beast branded us with its stare.

Just like Leery said it might.

"Whoa," Damon said.

It was then that I realized how heavy my legs felt. And the rest of my body, too. This was not good

news. The beast was doing all the bad stuff Leery warned us about. Sure, the tattoos would fade. But if we didn't get away from this creature soon, that eye on its tongue would come out and then the beast might blink us all to death!

"RUN!" I howled. "RUN FOR YOUR LIFE! FOR ALL OF OUR LIVES! DON'T LET THE MONSTER OPEN ITS MOUTH!"

We sped past the marble entryway in the library and through the wooden doors.

We zigzagged down the enormous set of stairs outside the library.

We began to race across the library lawn as fast as we could go.

The beast kept chasing us. It screamed, "RI RANT RY RYEBALL!"

And, just then, it hit me! "It's saying 'Give me back my eyeball!' That's all it is. It wants its eyeball back."

"Good call, Stella!" Lindsey said.

"DON'T STOP! KEEP RUNNING!" I cried to the other members of the squad. "It's fast but we can outrun it!"

The beast was gaining on us, though.

And it was about to catch up with San San.

"Go on without me," San San huffed. "I can't outrun the beast!"

She ducked behind a bush and we kept running. I hated leaving San San behind, but we had no choice. Luckily, the monster's eyes were trained on me. It still didn't realize that it was chasing after two versions of the woman from the movie.

"RIVE RE RACK RY RYEBALL!" the beast cried again, louder than before.

"Run faster!" I cried to the others.

At some point, somehow, we got way ahead of the beast. It was fast, but we were faster. We didn't have a thousand eyeballs to lug around.

We stopped for a second, and Lindsey turned around and aimed her zoom lens back to see what it would do next.

"Oh no!" Lindsey cried as she looked into the camera.

"Oh no what?" Damon yelled.

"The beast!" Lindsey said. "It looks upset! I think it's—oh no . . ."

"No!" I yelled. "Please tell me it's not—"

"Crying!" Lindsey said. "Tears are rolling out of every single eyeball!"

I remembered the flood scene from the movie.

But before I could even count to ten, a tidal wave

of monster tears whooshed our way. The surge came fast—too fast. There was no way to outrun this river. We held our breath as we got swept into the river current. It was a very good thing this beast's tears weren't poisonous . . .

What a ride! We bobbed along like corks, rushing with the water past some Riddle landmarks like the Drive-O-Rama parking lot and the old turbine windmills on Route 5. We tried to keep our heads above the tears, but it was hard work. I was grateful for all those extra swimming lessons last summer.

"Talk about drowning in your sorrows!" Lindsey cried out.

"Drowning would be kind of bad, wouldn't it?" Jesse said as his head went underwater.

"You think?" I gasped and gulped down a mouthful of the river. "Bleeeeech!" I cried.

"Yuck." Damon's head popped up. "This stuff tastes like dirt."

We each got swept under at least once, but somehow the river managed to pull us safely along the surface for the most part. I was scared we might hit rocks or barriers, but we didn't hit anything hard. I wondered if the good luck meant the eyeball amulet in my pocket was still working some kind of magic.

The river of tears began to narrow as it flowed down a hilly road. And then, without warning, it dumped us onto an abandoned lot. We flung our bodies onto dry land and wheezed. There was no sign of the B-Monster anywhere.

"That was the closest call the Monster Squad ever had!" Jesse cried.

Lindsey checked and her camera still worked. She snapped a photo of Damon and me on the ground.

"Are we really okay?" I asked, pinching myself.

Damon was too freaked out to say much of anything. Jesse was trying to figure out if the beast was still following us.

I stood up slowly and shook myself out. Thank goodness San San had ducked away before the river. She never would have made it!

"Look! The tattoos are fading!" Lindsey said, pointing to our arms.

Jesse pointed at my jeans. "Hey, Stella, the amulet faded, too. What's wrong with it?"

I looked down. The bright yellow shine from

inside my pocket was gone. The amulet wasn't sending a signal anymore.

We all glanced at each other, the same thoughts on our mind. No glow meant something important. Had the water done something to the B-Force? Or had the B-Monster disappeared again?

Where had the Eyeball Beast gone?

CHAPTER 12

TRANCE-LVANIA

Although we made it safely to shore, we had failed our Monster Squad mission.

The beast was still at-large.

We had to get back into downtown Riddle and find a way to outsmart the beast—before it was too late.

Some time had passed, so we figured the beast's powerful trance would have worn off Ms. Shenanigans and everyone else in town by now.

But we were so wrong.

The postman was sitting in his mail truck without moving.

A father and his daughter stood in front of a walkway even though the light had switched to green.

Someone's dachshund was frozen in mid-bark. Its mouth was wide open, but no sound came out.

People who had gathered on the town square lawn near the library looked like popsicles, frozen stiff in the middle of some picnic.

An Eyeball Beast trance had been expertly cast on all the residents of Riddle.

"This place has turned into Trance-lvania!" Lindsey said.

I wanted to cry my own river of tears. Poor Riddle. Poor San San.

And then, out of nowhere, San San showed up. She'd been safe behind that bush!

"Monster Squad!" San San cried out. She threw her arms around me. "I thought you kids would be washed away—but then

I realized you couldn't be washed away! You're the Monster Squad. While the beast was chasing you, I slipped into the drugstore to get some protective gear. I left a ten dollar bill on the counter since the cashier was frozen in his tracks."

San San pulled out a bag filled with mirrored sunglasses.

"I may be a feeble old woman, but I do know the Eyeball Beast. These mirrored glasses will help cover our eyes if we glance at it by mistake," San San said. "That's what we planned for the movie, anyway." We looked like Monster Squad Goes Hollywood in our mirrored glasses, not that it made a difference what we looked like since no one here could see us.

We looked up and down Main Street, searching for more signs of the beast. The only thing we found were more people and animals in trances.

"Wait!" San San said. "In the movie, Leery wanted to send the monster up Nerve Mountain!"

"You think that's where it's headed now?" I asked. Having San San here was so great! She knew more about the beast than anyone!

"Go and see," San San said. "I'll wait here by the library."

I started to walk away with the others, but then I stopped. The amulet in my pocket had begun to glow as brightly as fire—and it got just as hot.

"Oh no!" I said, turning around. "San San!"

But I was too late.

Towering behind my aunt was the Eyeball Beast! His eyeballs were dangling all over the place, blinking faster than I'd ever seen them blink before. The beast's eyeball arms reached down and scooped San San high up into the air.

"We have to help her!" I screamed, assuming one of my karate poses. "What are we going to do?"

The kick! Brick's kick! I gathered all my strength and leaped high into the air. But before I could make contact, the beast took off with San San.

"Don't worry!" San San wailed. "Follow us! Follow us!"

"Where?" I cried.

"NERVE MOUNTAIN!" Jesse, Lindsey, and Damon yelled at the same time.

We took off after the monster. But our legs couldn't move so fast. The monster moved like lightning up the side of the mountain. We could hardly keep up.

"I don't see it anywhere!" I cried.

"Wait! Use the amulet!" Jesse cried.

I yanked it out of my pocket. It was hot again—almost too hot to touch.

"I bet we can use it to follow him," Jesse said.

And then something dawned on me. All we really needed was to offer the amulet in exchange for San San!

"RIVE RE RACK RY RYEBALL!"

"Dirt!" Damon cried. He bent over on the mountain and rubbed his fingers in mud. When he poked his head up again, there was a dark smudge of black on his forehead. "It's like another eye—an *evil* eye—to make the monster go away! I read about it in one of the books I found this morning."

But before I had a chance to say anything, Lindsey took the words right out of my mouth. "We don't need dirt. We have the amulet! Let's just give it back to the beast and he'll give us San San!"

"That sounds too easy," Damon said.

We kept moving up the mountain. There were so many things to think of and do at once. I kept my eyes on the amulet's glow. We couldn't afford to lose the B-Monster again.

As we rose up over a bluff, I saw something I didn't expect to see so quickly. The Eyeball Beast had stopped! He was perched on a rock, eyes twitching. And on a rock next to the beast was San San!

Here was our chance!

CHAPTER 13

SNAP,
KICK, THRUST

"HERE IS YOUR EYEBALL!" I screamed.

The beast turned around, eyeballs twitching at us. He wasn't backing off.

"Say it again!" Lindsey cried.

"TAKE YOUR EYEBALL BACK!" I cried.

It still wasn't working. The beast didn't know what to make of us. Maybe he thought we were trying to trick him?

Then I spotted an empty cup on the ground and remembered something I had read at the library.

Defeat the power of the eye with a vessel of spit.
Collect human spit in a cup; then throw it on the
eye. The spit will destroy the curse—and the eye.

"Over here!" I commanded everyone to hide behind a rock so we could all spit in the cup.

"We need a lot of spit if we're going to get a thousand evil eyes," Lindsey said.

"Excellent! I love spit!" Damon said. He made a gross noise and then spit.

"Damon! Gross!" Lindsey said. But she spit, too.

Jesse spit a lot. "Quick thinking, Stella," he said, wiping his mouth and spitting again.

I passed the cup around and we spit until I felt certain we had enough to defeat the B-Monster. Carefully, I carried the cup up the mountain with us.

"Keep walking!" I yelled. The amulet was warming up again. "It's glowing!"

"Where did San San go?" Lindsey asked.

We scanned the immediate area for signs of struggle.

"WHOA!" Damon yelled. "Over there! She's on that other rock!"

My aunt was sprawled across a giant boulder. But why wasn't she moving? Was she sleeping? Oh no! Was she *dead*?

"San San!" I cried. I left the spit cup and raced over with the amulet. I wasn't going to let anyone mess with this ninja—or a member of this ninja's family. I needed the amulet's luck right now.

Before I could get to the boulder, something knocked me sideways. I went flying.

"AAAAAAAAAAAAAAAAAAAAGH!"

It was the Eyeball Beast!

He plowed into me and knocked me off my feet. The amulet flew out of my hands and disappeared in the underbrush. How would I get San San back without it—I was finished!

"STELLA!" the other Monster Squadders cried.

"Nobody messes with my aunt!" I screamed at the beast. "LEAVE US ALONE!"

The Eyeball Beast glanced at San San like it was going to grab her again. Then it looked at me like it might grab me! Then it looked back at San San!

"Rwo Ran Rans?" it asked.

"Kiiiiiya!" I yelped, striking a bolder pose. "I'm going to knock your eyeballs off one by one!"

The monster blinked.

I remembered San San's words to me: "Be brave."

I remembered Brick's fancy footwork.

And just like that, a fight was on.

"Take that!" I kicked up one leg and sliced at the air. Then, from behind the beast, Damon, Jesse, and Lindsey gathered with large sticks in their hands. I needed to distract the beast a little bit more as they approached. Then they took the long sticks and began poking some of the beast's one thousand eyes.

The monster squealed and flinched as the sticks went into eyeball after eyeball after eyeball. The beast's eyes all oozed this funny-smelling splurt. *Everything* about this B-Monster was gross—with a side of gross.

"Ewwwwwww!" Damon cried, stepping back after a few pokes. "What is this monster made of? It reeks!"

They continued poking at the other eyeballs like they were playing Whac-A-Mole. Eyeball juice sprayed all over. The monster stumbled around blindly; moaning. Its blinks were more random now.

I moved in closer and cut the air with my arms, just like karate class.

Chop. Chop. CHOP!

"Stella, over there!"

I shot a look back at Damon. He indicated a small mound at the side from where we stood. Just past the mound was the mountain edge. It must have been a thousand foot drop.

"Time for a *real* cliffhanger, eh?" Lindsey shouted out.

All at once, all the things I'd learned for the test to get my black belt, came rushing into my head. I saw Brick again, leaping into the air.

No more messing around.

Time to be a kicking machine.

WHAM! BLAM! KAZZAM!

My legs whizzed through the air like whirlybirds. I was fleet-footed and the monster didn't see me coming. He was slower now that a bunch of his eyeballs had been poked. I was able to trick him into going in the direction of the cliff's edge. Jesse and Damon were right there, poking even more of the beast's eyes.

He stood up tall, all eight feet of him and stretched his eyeball arms way up into the air. That monster still had fight in him—but so did I! Then I realized what he was *really* doing. He threw his head back and opened his jaw wide.

"Don't look, Stella!" Lindsey cried. "He's going to use the eye on his tongue!"

Damon and Jesse screamed. "Look away!"

But I didn't look away.

I looked right at that Eyeball Beast's crazy face, until he poked his tongue out and the most powerful eye on the planet looked right back at me.

It was a lot larger than the other eyes. The white part was bloodshot and it pulsed like a vein.

"DON'T LOOK!" the other members of Monster Squad wailed again. "STELLA, YOU DON'T KNOW WHAT YOU'RE DOING!"

But I knew *exactly* what I was doing.

SPLAT CITY

"Kiiiiiya!" I screamed and then I *really* let loose.

I leaped high into the air, as high as I'd ever leaped before for a spin twist kick. I just needed to see my target, just for a split second. All my energy, all my strength boosted me up. As I lurched forward, my feet made contact with the primary eye. It was a direct hit!

The monster flew backward through the air . . .

Over the mound . . .

And right off the mountain in a cloud of dust!

"NO WAY!" Damon and Jesse shouted in unison. "YOU DID IT!"

They ran over to the edge before I even got there.

Hundreds of feet below, the eyeball monster had crash-landed on a rock.

Splat City.

Lindsey put her arm around me like a real friend. Pretty soon, the four of us were standing there, arm in arm, hugging. Thank goodness no one got a picture of *that*.

"Do you think it's dead?" Damon asked.

On the ground, all around the Eyeball Beast, there were smushed, crushed, and smooshed eyes. A few twitched madly, as if they still worked. But, this beast was a goner. As dead as the rock it landed on.

"What's that?" Jesse cried.

Over to the side, a lone eyeball seemed to have detached from the beast. It pulsated like it might come to life. I remembered the jars of eyeballs in the castle. All it took was one eyeball to make another and then another. We couldn't risk it!

Jesse scrambled down the rocks with another stick.

"Take that!" Jesse cried, poking the runaway eyeball hard.

I looked away. All this monster-crushing splurt was making me woozy. I liked being the ninja and all that, but I was ready for all this B-Monster to go.

"Ding, dong, the beast is dead!" Lindsey sang to the tune of *The Wizard of Oz* song. "Ding, dong, the Eyeball Beast is deeeeeeaad!"

I believed them, but I wanted to be extra-certain this monster would not be coming back. So I ran back to get the spit cup. A little insurance wouldn't hurt anyone—except the beast, of course.

I hustled down the cliff, too, with the cup of our spit.

"Incoming!" I cried and poured the spit over the beast's quivering, dying body.

The whole thing evaporated into a fine, pink mist.

"That would have made a great ending for the original movie," a voice said from behind us. "Leery would be proud."

I turned to see Great Auntie San San stumbling toward us. She was alive and walking around! The trance had been broken for good!

"San San!" I cried. "What happened?"

"You saved the day, Monster Squad," Great Auntie San San said, looking at the beast on the rock. "That's what happened. You saved the day. And you saved *me*."

Except for a few bumps and bruises from her wild ride on the shoulders of the Eyeball Beast, San San was A-OK. We were all okay. Even after swimming down a river of tears and poking one thousand eyeballs up the mountainside—we survived.

"Kids, I found this on the ground over there," San San said, holding up the amulet. "I'm happy to say that it brought us good luck after all."

I took it from her, expecting the same amulet I'd had just a moment before. But now this amulet was cold. It wasn't glowing anymore. It had gone black.

"We have to tell Walter and Leery what's happened," Jesse said.

"Hey," Lindsey said, pointing across the mountainside where they stood. "We're practically at Leery Castle. Why don't we go there right now?"

I pulled out my cell phone and we dialed Walter Block. He told us to come over to the castle pronto.

"Wait!" Damon said. "We can't go talk to Walter yet. We still have to find the original reel."

We all sighed. "Drat," Lindsey said. "I was so busy worrying about the Eyeball Beast that I forgot about the reel!"

"It wasn't screened in my apartment," San San said. "Where else could it be?"

"What about the library? Ms. Shenanigans has a bunch of old reels," I said.

"I don't think so," Damon said. "I scanned her shelves when we were in the library. I didn't see it."

"Maybe it was screened in Antarctica where Oswald Leery is," Jesse suggested.

"Or not," Lindsey said.

"We can't give up!" I said. "We have to find that reel before the movie gets screened again."

"I don't know if I can face another Eyeball Beast attack," San San said.

"Neither can we!" all four members of the Monster Squad said at once.

CHAPTER 15

A REEL MESS

The castle was about a fifteen minute walk from where we'd destroyed the B-Monster. I've never been so happy to see a pair of Crabzilla gates in my entire life. Of course, San San wasn't sure about stepping inside the castle after all these years.

I could tell how nervous she felt.

The door was ajar. We have permission to go into the castle even when no one is there. It's one of those Monster Squad privileges we got when we signed on to this gig.

"Walter?" I called out as we entered the hallway.

"Caw! Caw!" Poe the crow swooped down and landed on my shoulder.

San San broke into a wide smile when she saw him. "Poe! My baby!" She explained how the crow had come on to one of the movie sets as a baby bird. She couldn't believe he was all grown up.

"I don't think Walter is here," Damon said. "Maybe he went to meet Leery in Antarctica?"

I made a face. "He has to be here. We just spoke with him on the phone, dummy."

"Don't call me dummy, *dummy*," Damon snarled.

I wasn't in the mood for a showdown with the Eyeball Beast *and* Damon Molloy in one day. So Poe and I went in search of the reel.

"Walter! Walter! We're back!"

Everyone followed, but we could not find him; even when we searched the lower level and called out at the top of our lungs.

Then I saw a shaft of light coming from the door marked VAULT.

"Hey!" Jesse cried, heading for the door. "Walter must be working in here—"

He pushed the door open wide. I glanced around the room. What a mess. Walter had all the reels pulled out again.

"Monster Squad, you're here! I was thrilled to get your call! You figured out a way to corner the beast! Congratulations!" Walter said.

We all looked at each other.

"Um . . . Walter, we killed the Eyeball Beast, but . . ."

"Where are my manners!" he cried out. "We should be celebrating! We must contact Dr. Leery at once! How fortunate that you destroyed B-Monster number three so close to the castle! Now, so we can celebrate together. I'll go hook up the live video—"

"Wait!" I cried. "Walter, there's something we need to tell you."

San San stepped into view now.

"Sandra!" Walter called out. "What are you doing here?"

"I came along for the ride," San San said. Then she and Walter embraced. They had been old friends, too, and were happy to see each other.

"Did you want to tell me about her?" Walter asked, pointing to San San.

"No," I stammered. "W-w-whhat I wanted to say was . . ."

"We don't have the reel yet," Damon blurted.

I knuckle-punched Damon's shoulder for telling before I could.

"Oh," Walter grimaced. "Hmmmm. No reel

destroyed? Hmmmm. That's most unexpected and unfortunate news. As you recall, Dr. Leery said that was one of the most important parts of this mission . . ."

We all stared at our sneakers. What else could we do?

"Let's dial up Dr. Leery, anyway," Walter said. "He and I had scheduled a phone meeting this afternoon. I know he will be happy to hear about the demise of the beast . . ."

"And disappointed to hear about the reel," I added.

"Now, now, Stella . . ." Walter patted my back. "He only wants to support you. After all, you four are doing his work."

But Walter's words didn't help. I still felt sick to my stomach. And I couldn't escape the feeling that all this was my fault. While we waited for the connection to Leery, the five of us (San San included) helped Walter tidy up the vault. On the table next to the projector was a pile without labels. Walter said he had been going through them one by one to search for the outtake footage.

"Have you watched all of these?" I asked aloud as I picked over the pile of mystery reels. Some of them looked familiar. Some not. It was like the pile we'd gone through the day we watched *The Beast with 1000 Eyes* . . .

"STELLA!" Damon yelled out. "Oh no . . . I think you need to see this!"

"What is it?"

Damon held up a reel in front of my nose. I stared at it closely.

The Beast with 1000 Eyes.

"So?"

He pointed to another sticker, below the title.

ORIGINAL REEL.

My throat clenched. My pulse quickened. My head reeled.

It was the reel I'd chosen just the other day. The reel we *watched*. Somehow a COPY label from *another* reel had gotten stuck onto my reel. The ORIGINAL sticker beneath it had been hidden from sight.

Oh no.

Without realizing it, *I* had unleashed the eyeball B-Monster.

Me!

"Nice one, Ninja," Damon said. He raised an eyebrow at me. "So this is all *your* fault!"

My cheeks turned four shades of purple. I looked over at Walter in a panic. I had to sit down.

Lindsey and Jesse just stared at me with blank expressions on their faces. No one knew what to say. What kind of a ninja was I? How could I stand tall as a Monster Squad member again? I'd never messed up anything so badly. I would probably be banished from Monster Squad forever and ever.

But then, in that moment, in that embarrassing moment, something happened that surprised me even more than a beast with one thousand gooey eyes.

My fellow Monster Squadders told me not to worry. They backed me up. Even Damon.

"Yo, Ninja, don't freak out. It's okay. We got the beast! We saved the day!"

"You cannot be hard on yourself," San San said to me. "Stella, perhaps your mistake unleashed the beast, but since then, you also have done many good things. You helped give me the strength to stop worrying. I'm no longer afraid to face my own monsters. I couldn't have done any of that without the Monster Squad—especially you!"

Jesse handed me the original reel of *The Beast with 1000 Eyes*.

"We'd better destroy this reel once and for all," he said. "You want to do the honors, Stella?"

I took the reel in my hand and began to pull out the tape. Then I glanced up at Poe, sitting on a shelf. Having a sharp-beaked crow in the castle was helpful at that moment. Poe was more than happy to help us tear into the reel, too. I tossed the film into the air. Poe caught some film in his beak.

"So long, Eyeball Beast!" Damon screeched as the film quickly unspooled off the reel. We cheered and stomped on the loose ends. Then we tossed the remains into a garbage bag.

"Finally!" I cried. "We killed the B-Monster. We destroyed the reel. *Now* we can call Leery."

We headed into the screening room for our big conversation with the one and only Oswald Leery—and maybe a penguin or two.

With Walter's help, Lindsey downloaded a whole mess of digital photos of the eyeball monster, the pink mist, and one extreme close-up of the amulet.

We had quite a story to tell.

Through the Antarctic static, Leery appeared on-screen again in his parka. It felt a little bit colder in the room when his image showed up. The iceberg behind him shone bright white and his breath was pure steam. It was cold there, for sure, but Leery spoke to us as warmly as ever.

"Another fine job, Monster Squad," he said. "I can't express enough thanks for all you've been doing to help destroy the B-Monsters on the loose. Because of your brave actions, Riddle is a whole lot safer. Slimo, Mega Mantis, and now . . . the Beast with 1000 Eyes. I am impressed."

Then, from behind me, Great Auntie San San pushed forward a little bit closer to the screen.

"Oswald," she said meekly.

"SANDRA? Is that you?" Leery recognized San

San's voice right away. He got this weird expression on his face.

I was about to explain why San San was there, but Great Auntie San San placed her hand on my arm gently to let me know she'd handle this on her own.

"Yes, it is me, Oswald. Sandra Lee. My niece found me and asked me to help out. Yes, I know about your little experiment. You have assembled a team of champions, Oswald. It reminds me of our days together making the movies . . ."

I got a little concerned because Leery wasn't saying anything. His expression was expressionless.

"Walter," I whispered, "can you get more of a close-up on Leery? What's he doing?"

Walter zoomed in. We all let out a little gasp. Leery's face appeared frozen from the cold—but he was crying! Each teardrop turned to little icicles on his cheek.

"I'm so sorry, Sandra," Leery said. "I know how hard it has been all these years, keeping my secrets. I am sorry for putting you through that. And I am grateful for your help."

San San smiled. "Just how many of these B-Monsters are on the loose in Riddle anyway, Dr. Leery?" she asked.

Leery smiled back. "One at a time! That's about all we can handle!"

"Oh no!" Damon let out a wail. He pointed to the screen. "Over there! Behind Leery! It's another B-Monster—coming up from the water!"

I squinted to see exactly what Damon was talking about. Then I let out a laugh.

"That's no monster! That's a seal!" I said.

We all chuckled. Then San San took her hand in mine and stood close to the microphone so Leery could hear as clearly as possible. She apologized to Leery for stealing the amulet from the set of the movie. She wanted to give back the relic after all these years, but Leery wouldn't take it. He insisted that San San keep it. It was, he said, a part of a B so it belonged to the Queen B.

All at once, my cell phone rang in my pocket. I checked the display. It was my alarm again, reminding me of something important.

KARATE MEET.

I nearly screamed.

Karate? Karate! I had almost forgotten about it. The most important meet of my life was in just one hour! I needed to get back to Dojo Academy pronto!

We said our good-byes—for the time being—to Leery.

Then Walter volunteered to drive all of us down Nerve Mountain to the karate studio.

CHAPTER 16

RUNNER-UP, UP, AND AWAY

Competition day at Dojo Academy was a real blur. I think this was partially due to the fact that I was dog tired. What a week it had been! I'd met a long-lost aunt, tracked down and destroyed the beastly Eyeball Beast, and found a glowing amulet with monstrous powers.

But I had to shake off my nerves and tired bones. It was time to compete.

I spotted Brick and his family right away and waved. Then I saw my own family in the viewing gallery. Mom waved. I'd called her earlier to let her know that I was spending the morning with my friends and I'd meet her at Dojo Academy. I'd also told her that I had bumped into someone she knew and that person would be coming to the meet, too.

As soon as we arrived, Front Desk Lady pulled

together another row of chairs for the members of the Monster Squad, Walter, and my surprise guest, San San.

When I brought Great Auntie San San over to Mom, they just stared at each other for a moment. And then they slowly started to talk. *Whew. That was easier than I thought.*

Now all I had to do was kick my way to a black belt. No sweat. I headed back into the karate studio to do some warm-up exercises. Wouldn't Brick be surprised when he saw me do his kick for the judges?

As it turned out, Brick was in rare form. Sure, he made fun of osu during practice, but he used it perfectly during our match. He pinned me on the floor and knocked me off the mats more than once.

Eventually, I landed flat on my back, with Brick standing over me.

"Tough break, Ninja," Brick said. He helped me up. "Better luck next time."

I got up and waved to the Monster Squad, Walter, San San, and Mom. Everyone was clapping. But despite losing, I did not feel like a runner-up. I was a winner—all-around. I helped kick some monster butt and I got to know my long-lost aunt. I even got a trophy, never mind that it was only for second place. If all this wasn't winning, then what was?

Brick came over to me after the awards had been distributed and I was sure he'd gloat some more. After all, his trophy was three times the size of mine.

"See you in class next week?" he asked.

This day was certainly full of surprises. "Next week!" I said.

"So who's up for a great big barbecue tomorrow?" Mom asked as we strolled out of Dojo Academy. "Auntie San San already said she'll be there. And your friends are all welcome!" she said, pointing to Lindsey, Jesse, and Damon.

They looked back at me.

"Friends?" Damon cracked.

But the truth was, it was getting harder and harder not to consider my fellow squad members as actual true friends.

"Hey, Stella," Jesse said. "Let me see your trophy."

I handed it over. The engraving on the bottom read:

STELLA MIN

KYU 2

DOJO ACADEMY

"For what it's worth," Jesse said to me, "I think you were number kyu one, not kyu two. Whatever that word means."

"And as far as *I'm* concerned," Damon added, "you really are a ninja."

As we walked outside, the sky looked ominous, like a storm was blowing in. Night was coming, too. *Brrrrr.* I shoved my hands into my pockets to shake off the chill.

Mom and San San stood off to the side, saying their good-byes.

Lindsey stood off to the other side, snapping photos in the half dark. The flash kept going off like a strobe light. I posed like a ninja, of course, for as many photos as possible. Damon pretended to be a ninja standing next to me. He was good for comic relief sometimes.

In the midst of our photo session, Jesse whispered, "Hey, guys, what's that up there? Up in the sky? Do you see something?"

Jesse, Lindsey, Damon, and I all looked straight up toward the looming clouds. There was a strange flying object way off in the distance behind a cluster of trees. Was it a plane? It hovered near

Nerve Mountain, almost like it was hanging over Leery Castle. Were they birds? It looked a little like a ship.

"I don't know what that is," Damon stammered. "But that thing is not from around here!"

"Could it be some kind of UFO?" Lindsey asked.

"Whoa," Damon blurted.

Before we could take a second look, the mystery object vanished back into the sky.

San San came over. "You four look like you just saw a ghost!" she said.

I shrugged. "Um . . ." I wasn't sure what to tell her.

"Maybe you four will let me in on your next B-Monster adventure?" she asked.

"Maybe," I swallowed hard. "As long as it doesn't involve any eyeballs."

LOOK OUT FOR BOOK 4:
THEY CAME FROM PLANET Q